#3

Beryl E. Bean

Adventure: Lonely Leader

By Ricki Stern and Heidi P. Worcester

Illustrations by Amy June Bates

HarperCollinsPublishers

CHAPTER ONE
HURRICANE ALEX:
A NATURAL DISASTER

I

Berry E. Bean

MAPster
(Mighty Adventurer of the Planet)
am on a MAPmission: Lose the Loser. The Loser
(AKA—also known as—Alex Jordan) is the son of my mom's old
college roommate, Edith.

The Loser and his family live—or I should say LIVED—in a foreign country until two weeks ago, when the country decided it didn't like being ruled by a dictator. A dictator is like a bossy parent telling you what to do all the time. So the people had a revolution.

Hmm, I wonder if I could stage a revolution against my mom. BAN THE BROCCOLI! LIVER MUST LIVE!! FREE FRIED FOOD!!!

To protect Alex, his parents have DUMPED him on my turf until they can get all their stuff shipped back to the Big Apple (AKA New York City). Usually, I welcome the unexpected, but Alex invaded like a mosquito on a naked ankle. I am waaaay too busy to play host! I have been working around the clock with my teammate—my best friend M.P.—on MY campaign for Spring Leader. Spring Leader is like being class president for the rest of the year.

Every spring each class gets to do a special project. This year my class will clean up—and transform, presto! magico!—the lot next door to the school. As Spring Leader, I will get to decide what we transform the lot and all the rot into.

Rot makes me think of Alex. He is like fruit roll-ups. They appear sweet and harmless—*all natural*—but if they stick to your teeth, they rot right through them. The first day Alex was here, I caught him taking Fragrant Fanny, my guinea pig, out of her cage, without so much as a hello, please, or may I. So of course I investigated.

WHO said you could hold Fanny?
And WHY are you holding her?

Nosy, aren't you?

Not nosy. Inquisitive. I'm a
`Mighty Adventurer of the Planet.`
I was born to ask questions.

An adventurer?

A MAPster. I seek adventure and explore the questionable.

I'm an adventurer too. I visited eight countries in two years. I bet your greatest accomplishment was getting eight cavities in two years.

Don't try to change the subject.
Unhand Fanny.

Chill, Ms. Mighty Galaxy! I was just holding your rodent.

Uh, duh! I can see that. WHY?

Uhhh . . . I was evaluating whether or not this animal would make a tasty dinner for my python, Prince William.

You were going to feed my fluffy Fanny to your slimy reptile!? Murderer.

Of course, when I told my mom about Alex's depravity, she said he was joking and I needed to be more sensitive to *HIS feelings.* Warren, my stepdad, laughed, saying Alex was only teasing and trying to be friends. Then Warren reminded me that a MAPster would `Look for the upside: MAPster rule # 1.` Looking for the upside of Alex was like looking for a beauty mark on a freckled person—challenging! But then I came up with one: Alex is a boy, so he gets stuck sharing my little brother, Kevin's, bedroom, smelly sock capital of the world!

After the python incident, I was on my guard—and a good thing too! I've been keeping track of Alex's deception in my MAPpad. Observe!

MY FAMILY IS DUPED!

1) Alex convinced Kevin to be happy he's sleeping in Kevin's trundle bed by telling him the boogey man will get Alex first, leaving Kevin time to escape. Manipulative!

2) Warren is "thrilled" to have a new face in the house. (What's the matter with my OLD face?)

3) Alex told my mom that she made the best sandwiches ever just so she would get up extra early to pack him his "EXOTIC" Nutella-and-guava-jam croissant sandwiches. Tricky.

4) Normally, I wouldn't care who my stepsister, Lulu, likes, but when she let Alex use her triple-powered, multihead shower massage because he said her hair smelled like a country-fresh morning—that was more than I could handle!

Barf-o-rama!

Kevin may have to share his room with Alex, but I have to share my classroom. Through a little finagling my mom was able to get Alex into my class mid-year. There goes my last inch of personal space. My classmates are so bored with each other that Alex has become a mini-celebrity overnight. He's always got an audience for his stories.

So then I ducked behind a tree when a baby rhino charged me, missing my left cheek by a fraction of a hair.

Cool, wow, Dudeman, All hail King of the Rhinos!

Well, my family is part ROYALTY.

Yeah, a ROYAL pain.

Can you believe no one laughed but me?!

To Do List
Investigate Alex's lineage.
Ask Mom: Alex = Royalty???
Doubtful!!!

Alex has taken center stage with everyone except M.P. Even though she thought it was cool when he tie-dyed his shirt with cranberry juice at lunch, she's still devoted to my cause.

M.P. isn't just my best friend! She's a
Mighty Adventurer of the Planet,
too, which means I can always count on her to explore the unknown and pursue the perilous! (Unless she has piano practice.)

For two weeks M.P. and I have been hanging campaign posters and handing out twig pencils printed with my name.

Beryl for Spring Leader
She springs to the lead!

BERYL BEAN

Mr. Joel, our totally cool homeroom teacher and ex–pro surfer, thinks my campaign shows the "tubular imagination and stellar skill needed to be a leader"—and to change the world! (I added that.) Plus, Mr. Joel loves my Rainforest Crunch cookies wrapped in recycled (it was only used once) tinfoil.

The election is tomorrow. So far, I'm the only candidate. If no one runs against me, I'll be declared the winner. Once I'm Spring Leader, I'll inspire such dedication that Alex will be like a shadow on a cloudy day—INVISIBLE.

CHAPTER TWO
ELECTION DAY
(AKA VOTE-FOR-BERYL DAY!)

Tuesday morning, my jaw hits the floor. There on the wall of our classroom is a poster.

Alex is beginning to feel like a marathon case of the hiccups. Annoying! Time to confront the competition face-to-face.

So what are your great ideas for transforming the lot and changing the world?

They are so great, I wouldn't want to spoil the surprise.

Oh, I think I can handle it. Let the competition begin!

Flattery will get you nowhere. I'd hardly call it a competition.

At recess, I grab M.P. for an emergency meeting by the lockers.

Anybody who knows me KNOWS I was born to be Spring Leader. I'm a natural. Get it? I'd recycle toilet paper if I could!

Yuck.

All Alex knows how to do is follow. Our class needs a leader and I have the most potential to lead.

But you have the least potential to listen. Part of being a good leader is listening.

I hear you.

Remember when I said we could make an orchestra space and use the garbage in the lot to make soda can mariachis and paper towel holder rain sticks? You didn't even listen, Beryl. You were kinda bossy.

Bossy? Bossing? Being the boss! Isn't that what leaders do? As I bang my locker shut, I see Alex scurry around the corner. Hmmm, I thought I smelled a rat.

After recess, Mr. Joel blows his conch shell, which means listen up.

The Spring Leader competition has heated up with Alex Jordan's last-minute entry. AWESOME. So let's allow Beryl and Alex to take a moment each to show us their goods. Then we'll vote and crown the victor.

The class chants:

SPEECH! SPEECH! SPEECH!

Before Alex can STEAL the limelight, I jump onto my chair and motion for silence.

Why choose me for Spring Leader? Environmental pollution is a serious problem. Mary, every time you flush the toilet you use 5 gallons of water. Raja, the wrapper on your Twinkie takes 400 years to biodegrade. Lucy, your purple hair spray is breaking down the ozone layer. I know how to make the earth a better place. I will transform the lot from a heap of trash to a mountain of possibilities. Vote B for Better, Best, BERYL.

Alex unveils a drawing of the abandoned lot with a large question mark in the middle. DRAT! Visual aids!

I believe the lot should be what YOU all want it to be. Let's say you like music, how about we, uhhh, make an orchestra from the lot's tin cans and empty oil drums? Or if you like art, we could make junk sculptures. I may not have all the global facts like Beryl, but I have been around the globe. Pitch in and we can work together and use all our ideas to make a difference! The more brains, the more gains!

Thief! He stole M.P.'s idea. Too late to do something about it. It's time to vote.

Mr. J. counts the votes and we write in our journals. While I'm doodling pictures of myself as victor reigning over Alex, Mr. J. toots his conch.

It's a tie!
Looks like we have two big kahunas. By Thursday, Alex and Beryl will share their plan for the abandoned lot with us. Go forward, class, and do great things!

Everyone gets up in slow motion, like oil moving through water. Suddenly, Alex is shaking my hand, calling me co-leader. I say quietly, "Leader means the boss and cannot be preceded by CO. It's an oxymoron! Moron." Alex smiles, saying, "Takes one to know one." Only I hear him.

Oxymoron: You know, two words that don't go together, like a fun test.

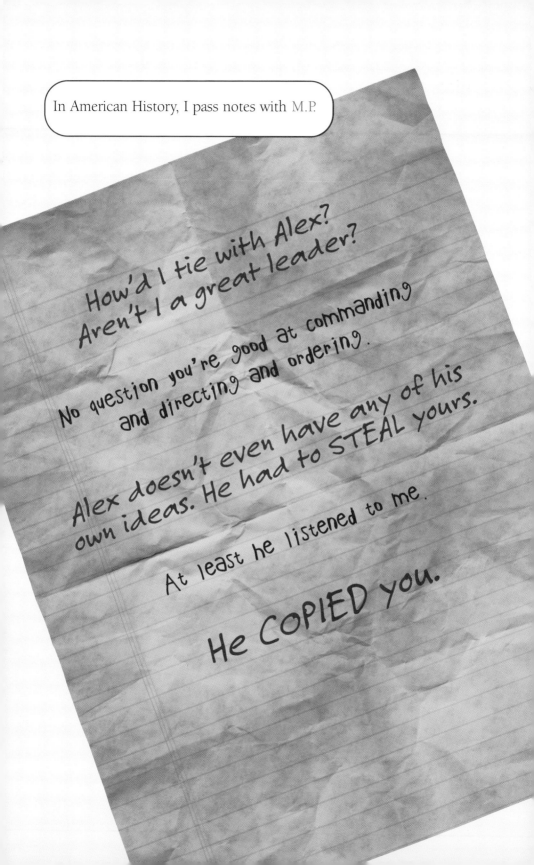

I feel like the lone witness to a crime. After class, I ask M.P. if she still wants to be on my team. If she's with me, I tell her she can help me work on ideas for the abandoned lot.

Alex is staying after school to do "*something*." At last, alone! Peace and tranquility on the streets of New York City. When I get home, Warren's head appears from around his office door.

How was the election?

Rotten. I'm sharing leadership with my nemesis.

You and Alex are co-leaders?

Is there an echo in here?

There must be an upside. Two heads are better than one.

Says who? The double-headed android?

I duck into my room and stay there until M.P. comes over. Warren orders a small *exotic* pizza with anchovies and capers for Alex and a medium plain for M.P. and me. Then M.P. and I escape to my room.

   I grab my **MAP**pad and start sketching. First I try out M.P.'s idea for an orchestra space. Then I start sketching MY fantabulous idea for an obstacle course—EVERYONE loves a playground—when there's a sudden rattle at the door and Alex walks in.

End
X

Start

truck
Stop

tired
of
tires

wall
challenge

jungle
gym

army
crawl

Obstacle Course
BERYL BEAN

Don't mean to intrude, but I was wondering if
we could swap ideas.

Don't you mean **swipe** my ideas? If you want to
share ideas, let's hear yours first.

When we lived in Botswana, our hut was decorated with
paintings of lions. Maybe the lot's wall would look cool
with a mural of aminals, I mean an-i-mals.

An an-i-mal mural? That's sooo original. That's what
the kindergarten class has on their wall.

Forget it!

Alex stomps out of my room, slamming the door behind him.

Spy!

He wasn't spying. He's the co-leader.
A mural might be cool.

Whose side are you on?

No one's.

Soooo you're not on my side.

That's not what I said.

That's what I heard.

What's up with you?

M.P. puts on her backpack and leaves without even saying good-bye. I hang a CLOSED sign on my door and build a comforter tent over two chairs. I crawl inside with a flashlight, some Milk Duds, and my MAPpad. I can't believe I just had a fight with my best friend. I have to prove to M.P. that Alex is a fake and a copy-cat. I cross out `Lose the Loser` and write: `MAPmission: Reveal the Rat`. I start listing the evidence.

MAPnotes
(To be investigated further!!!)

Petting
Fragrant Fanny?
= Doubtful

Staying after school?
= Secretive

Stealing friends?
= Blatant

CHAPTER THREE
SETTING THE RAT TRAP

At 6:30 the next morning, I wake to a noise in the hall. I open the door a crack. It's Alex, fully dressed.

I creep toward the kitchen where I hear a rustling sound. Alex is emptying out MY box of organic Sugar Balls cereal into a plastic bag. He puts the bag back in the cabinet and starts to leave with the box. Thief! The floor creaks and Alex looks up. I'm not sure if he saw me, so I slide quietly back down the hall and jump into bed. I fall back to sleep wondering WHAT Alex was up to and WHY he took my cereal box but left the cereal. The next thing I know, my mom is shaking me awake.

If Alex is stealing, Warren will know how to expose him. As soon as I'm dressed I make a beeline to his office. I'm about to deliver our secret **MAP**knock, when I hear Alex's voice from inside.

The queen is on her last leg. One more attack and she'd have been gone for good.

Meet me this afternoon at 3:30 downstairs in the lobby. I think I know someone who can take care of her.

Last leg? Queen? Take care of her? ME? The door swings open and Alex rushes past me.

Then Warren pokes his head out.

Beanster! Just the MAPster I was hoping to find lurking outside my office. I have a mission and I need your help. Meet me this afternoon at 3:30 in the lobby. I could use a friend.

A friend or a foe?

I call it MAPmission: Befriend a Friend.

Who's the friend?

That's for you to figure out.

Warren doesn't realize I overheard him. He and Alex are up to something and I'm going to find out what!

MAPmission: Double Agent commences!

At school, I notice M.P. is NOT wearing her rainbow friendship bracelet—the one we swapped gum over and SWORE we'd never take off, even if she gets asked to be a flower girl at her aunt's wedding. I shove MY bracelet DEEP into my pocket and avoid her. At lunchtime, I follow Alex to the library. When I catch up to him he is at the back of the stacks hunched over some papers. I sneak closer and spy a green notebook in front of him. It looks *verrrry* familiar. Fresh evidence! Time for a confrontation.

Alex, that's Mr. Joel's green notebook with the surfboard stickers! **Did you steal it? Are you cheating?**

I am not.

Then how come you have his notebook?
And why haven't you handed in your homework?

He gave it to me. I'm . . . Oh, forget it.
You won't listen to me anyway!

Why should I listen to a liar?

I add the discovery to my **MAP**notes.

Cheating on a reading assignment?
=
LIAR

Mission: Reveal the Rat closing in for success. Now if I can just expose Alex for the faker he really is, then I can regain full power and the throne! (Well, become the sole Spring Leader at least.) Warren's dubious mission this afternoon will give me the perfect opportunity to document Alex in action—and prove to everyone else what I already know. This time I'll be prepared.

CHAPTER FOUR
BLINDSIDED BY A SPARROW

After school, I rush home and
pack my MAPvest with
double-agent supplies:

Whistle
(for catching Alex in the act)

Mini-Instamatic camera
(for documenting hard evidence)

Vitamin C cherry sours
(to fortify brain power)

Strawberry Delicious bubble gum
(peace offering—double
agents need to pretend
to befriend the enemy)

Dark glasses
(if eyes are the
windows of the
soul, I don't want Alex
looking into mine)

Paper and indelible ink pen
(for Alex's confession)

I pop a vitamin C cherry sour and meet Alex and Warren at 3:30 in the lobby. Alex is carrying *MY* Sugar Balls box.

Smile for the camera. My first piece of evidence— red-handed with my cereal box.

Alex carefully hands me the Sugar Balls box. A little orange beak peeks out.

I've been feeding the birds in the park near Mrs. Grimaldi's dry cleaner's. Yesterday, I found this one struggling to fly. Her nest was destroyed. I named her Queen Cleo after my aunt Cleo who broke her arm climbing Mount Kilimanjaro.

Alex thinks her wing might be broken, which is why we're off to meet Dr. Darling. She's the head of the ornithology department at the Central Park Zoo.

Birds? Zoo? Interesting! On the bus, I pull out my **MAP**pad and add my new evidence.

MAPnotes
(To be investigated further!!!)

Petting Fragrant Fanny?
= Doubtful

Staying after school?
= Secretive

Stealing friends?
= Blatant

Cheating on a reading assignment?
= Liar

Getting up early to feed birds?
= CURIOUS

We get to the zoo, and before I can say AVIARY Warren hands Alex a map and takes off to do some research for his Hawk Girl interactive website. We will meet him back at the front gate at 5:30. Alone with the enemy!

If we hurry, it looks like we'll catch the penguin feeding at, uhhhh, 4:05. They're one of the FEW bird species I haven't seen in my travels.

NEXT
FEEDING 4:50

After five minutes of walking, we end up at the rest rooms. I grab the map from Alex.

You said LEFT when we should have gone RIGHT! But, don't sweat it, Alex. We're a team. Have a piece of Strawberry Delicious bubble gum.

Double agents, start your engines! We backtrack and pass by the penguins. The sign says Next Feeding at 4:50—not 4:05. It's not for another 45 minutes. I snap a photo and make a note on my MAPpad: Very Fishy. I don my dark glasses and lead us the rest of the way to Dr. Darling's office without a hitch.

Dr. Darling's desk sits in the center of a round room ringed by birdcages. After introducing ourselves, Alex hands her the Sugar Balls box. Dr. Darling chirps a birdsong to Cleo.

Our friend has a fractured wing. See these puncture wounds? Sparrows are territorial. When other birds invade their space, they feel threatened and become defensive. It looks like this one was probably defending her home from an intruder.

I can relate. Hmm, I wonder if I'll end up with puncture wounds.

Here's what we will do. While I go find some tape for her wing, you two promising ornithologists can prepare a topical antibiotic to prevent infection.

She puts out the ingredients and instructions. Alex takes Cleo out of the box, gently stroking her head. He looks almost tender as he nestles her into a towel, then he starts to mix the medicine.

What are you doing—trying to poison Cleo? You've mixed too much antibiotic into the cream. You are evil.

I didn't do it on purpose.

Oh really! It's just like when I caught you cheating in the library! The minute anyone turns her back, you become the double, dirty—

Dyslexic! I have dyslexia! Okay?

Dyslexia?
Is that some rare disease you caught traveling?

Forget it! Not that you would care . . . dyslexia is not a disease and it's not contagious. It just means sometimes I get things backward. Okay?

I noticed.

My brain works great on some things, but it takes longer for me to learn things, like reading, than the average person like you. That's why Mr. Joel lent me his notebook!

Hey, I wouldn't call me average.

Average is way better than different, believe me. It's twice as hard for me to do some things.

Like speaking in front of a lot of people makes me want to barf. I'm so nervous I'll mess up.

Gross. So then why did you run against me for leader?

Because you were ignoring me!

Because everyone else was paying attention to you!

Only because I listen to them and you don't!!! *But who cares? If they find out I'm dyslexic they'll just think I'm stupid. It's always the same. You can have your friends back. I'd rather hang out with animals. They never desert me.*

Dr. Darling appears, and Alex turns his back to me. Alex holds Cleo while Dr. Darling finishes mixing the cream, rubs it on Cleo's wing, then tapes it down so she looks like a mummy. She tells Alex she'll have to keep Cleo under close observation while the wing heals. Looks like Alex is being dumped again.

On the bus home, I stick my nose deep into my **MAP**pad and amend my **MAP**notes while Warren tells Alex about designing the Hawk Girl interactive website.

MAPnotes
(To be investigated further!!!)

Petting Fragrant Fanny?
= ~~Doubtful~~ = Lonely

Staying after school?
= ~~Secretive~~ = Extra help

Stealing friends?
= ~~Blatant~~ = Alone

Cheating on a reading assignment?
= ~~Liar~~ = Needed help and extra time

Getting up early to feed birds?
= ~~CURIOUS~~ = Animal lover

CHAPTER FIVE
IN THE DUMPS

When we get home, I go directly to my room. I failed **Mission: Befriend a friend**, and **Mission: Reveal the Rat** turned out to mean I AM THE RAT! All this time, I, Beryl E. Bean, was blinded by the green-eyed monster—JEALOUSY.

Time for this leader to lead. I start to call M.P., but then remember she isn't talking to me. My new mission is simple. **Mission: Apologize.**

...ch the empty lot incorporating Alex's and M.P.'s ideas ... orchestra space and my idea for an obstacle course. I make a copy for Alex and leave it by his door with a note on strawberry scratch 'n sniff paper. My favorite!

Dear Alex,

Sorry we started off so crazy. If I'd known you were dyslexic, I wouldn't have tried so hard to beat you. Leave it all to me and check out the sketch. Don't worry, we can be co-leaders, but I'll handle the hard stuff.

Beryl

I wake up refreshed and ready to embrace Alex. We'll be partners 50/50. Well, maybe 51/49. I'm about to skip to breakfast when I spy a note stuck to my door by a wad of *my* Strawberry Delicious bubble gum.

Why'd I expect you to be different? You don't have to worry about me messing things up on your project. I'll be too busy finishing the reading homework! I quit.
Alex

Who does he think he is quitting on ME? I'm the one who's supposed to be making decisions around here.

In homeroom, Mr. J. announces that Alex is withdrawing as co-leader. I quickly thwart the groans by posting a large drawing of my plans for the lot.

Voilà! Here it is. The moment we've all been waiting for . . . drum roll please . . . our class project. It is a FUSION of many ideas. Over here is an obstacle-course playground and over here we'll clear a space for concerts. It will be a place to strengthen the mind and body. One last and most IMPORTANT thing, I've assigned everyone JOBS for Saturday.

I pass out copies of the job list, then station myself at the black-board. Strangely, nobody looks at me. I move over to M.P.

The music space looks cool, huh?

What made you think I'd be good at weeding?

Whatever happened to a big fat "Gee, thanks, Beryl, for incorporating my idea into your plan"?

I start to tell her about my new MAPster rule: #4: "Complain. No gain." But she rolls her eyes. Then Mr. Joel tells me that for the next two days I'll be working full throttle preparing for the class project. I'll need to get together all the supplies from the school's art room, maintenance storage, and cafeteria. He asks for volunteers to help me. No hands go up, not even a pinky. He wisely decides volunteering is overrated and assigns me some assistants.

CHAPTER SIX
A LOT TO DO

Two days later, I've put Mission: Apologize on the back burner, which is fine because Alex seems suddenly to be MIA (missing in action) and M.P. is treating me like yesterday's underwear. And after lugging workclothes, cleaner, and brooms up two flights from maintenance, my assistants have decided assisting is over-rated! On Friday night, I've got lots of last-minute work so I recruit Kevin to help. But after five minutes of sorting garbage bags, he throws his Snickers wrapper on the floor and leaves saying, "Wow! Helping keep the world clean can make a person thirsty."

I confess! I am in need of **MAP**ster help. I look for Warren and find him in his office reading the newspaper and dripping bits of his egg-and-jelly sandwich down his shirt.

Caught me!

I'm not here to expose your gross habits. I need some help as Spring Leader.

You wanted to be sole captain of the ship. What's up?

There's been a mutiny—as in rebellion. I need a system for getting everything accomplished. Any suggestions, Sir MAPster?

My suggestion: Go ask your ex-co-leader.

Alex? Why him? Anyway, why would he want to help me?

Maybe because you NEED him.

But he's a quitter. Besides, he's dyslexic and things are too hard for him.

I know he's dyslexic. But you seem to forget that leaving his home was hard, moving to a new school was hard, trying to make friends with you was week-old-bread-rock HARD. He's worked at those things and hasn't quit. Having dyslexia doesn't mean he is stupid, Beryl.

You're right. I'm the one who is stupid. There, I've said it! And furthermore, I admit I could really use Alex as a co-leader. Phew! I'm feeling much, much better. But big whup, I still can't change his mind. Can I?

May I offer up MAPster rule #5: The best way to win over your opponent is to put yourself in his cleats. *Think about it, Beryl.*

What would make *me* want to help ME? Hmmmmmm. Ahhhhh. Errrrrrrrrr. Brain surge! Bingo! I pick some egg off Warren's shirt and quickly go to draw up a plan for the lot that illustrates Alex's animal-mural idea in eye-popping, full-fluorescent color. Once Alex sees the mural, he'll know I think it's cool and he'll have to help. By the time I finish, I am zonked. I quietly leave a copy for Alex outside his door and flop onto my bed to catch some Zs.

6:00 A.M. Saturday morning, I'm EXHAUSTED, but I'm ready! As Warren helps me into the elevator with a shopping cart full of Milk Duds and icy cold Grape Fizzberry soda (which cost me the last of my savings but will hopefully appease my class), Alex passes us on his way in from feeding the birds.

Alex, umm, I've coined MAPster rule #6 after you: The greater brains, the greater gains. I could really use your brain today.

Brain? You can't be talking about me. You must mean b-r-a-W-n—not b-r-a-I-n.

He closes the door. Now he's deserting ME! Didn't he see my new plan for the lot?

Gulp! At the lot, reality strikes. The lot looks like a trash tornado hit and caused major destruction, and the other fifth graders don't exactly look thrilled to be there. I summon reserve energy and run around handing out rubber gloves, goggles, and garbage bags, trying to psych everyone up . . . including me. I put on my most enthusiastic voice.

Okay, people, this is not going to happen on its own. Weeders! Get down on your knees! Garbage collectors! Stop yacking! Start collecting! Okay, gardeners! Dig! Plant! Water! It's that simple!

Even after I break out the Milk Duds and Grape Fizzberry soda, things are still going disastrously! Laura Kinks doesn't want to handle garbage, but Joe Smalls says it's got to be better than weeding. He's quitting. I give Joe Laura's job and shift Laura to clipping. Then I reassign M.P. to sandwich making but handling cold cuts gives M.P. the willies, so I switch her to raking, but then she says she can't risk a blister or her piano instructor will have a hissy. There is no one to strategize with because nobody is talking to anybody—especially not to me. A dark shadow falls over me.

Being a dictator can be a lonely job.

Alex? I thought you had to catch up on reading.

I think I can finish it tomorrow with a little help. Hint, hint.

Deal. Before you say anything, I apologize a google times over. Thanks for showing up.

Thank Cleo. Once her wing heals, she'll need a new place to live. I figured I should help fix up her new home. I'm going to paint her picture on the animal mural.

So you like MY idea.

I think you mean MY idea.

Touché, YOUR idea for the mural. Now get to work.

Is that an order?

Sorry, I mean let's get to work.

Alex bangs a shovel on a garbage can lid, and before I can say "don't barf" he is up on a barrel commanding the troops.

Attention! Umm class, this is OUR project and if it fails then we all fail! But if we work together, then we ALL succeed! So forget your assigned job. Figure out how YOU want to make a difference. Then go and do it!

The grumbling slowly stops. M.P. takes charge of the boom box and starts weeding to some loud opera lady. Alex and I set up an assembly line, making 60 peanut-butter-and-jelly and baloney-on-wheat sandwiches in 15 minutes flat. `Mission: Apologize` on the road to success!

At lunch I find M.P. sunning herself. I pull out our friendship bracelet and put it back on.

No response. I try another approach.

Strawberry Delicious bubble gum? I should have listened to my fellow MAPster when you said I was bossy. Sometimes you know me better than I know me. I was a tiny, eensy bit jealous and thought I should be the sole, lone leader but I ended up ALONE without anyone to lead. Simply put—I stink, stank, stunk! I'm sorry.

If you'd only listened to me I would have followed you.

You're totally RIGHT-eous! I promise to shut up and listen—at least for the rest of the day.

M.P. cuts off a plastic soda can circle and slips it onto her wrist. Then we raise our Grape Fizzberries and toast to friendship.

At the end of the day, the lot looks great! I stand on an abandoned couch and tell the class about Alex's stupendous, tremendous, fantabulous idea for an animal mural. Arianna practically hyperventilates she's so excited to paint a portrait of her miniature poodle, FiFi (short for French Fry). The class votes. It's unanimous. We will come back Monday during free period to paint. I survey the lot and picture the mural. Gee, I wonder if there are nontoxic paint thinners, biodegradable paint sticks, and ozone-safe spray paint? Ahh, saving the world is a 24-7 job!

Just then Mr. Joel blows his conch a final time and we follow him to the Pie in Your Eye pizza parlor, famous for its 100 organic toppings. At the restaurant, he hands Alex and me the menu, saying the co-leaders have the honor of reading aloud the toppings. I stand up quickly to save Alex from embarrassment and begin to read artichokes, anchovies, asparagus. When I get to capers, carrots, and crushed pineapple, Alex interrupts.

Hey, stop hogging the menu.

It's okay, Alex. I can handle this alone.

I know it can be hard for you to share the spotlight, but I am the co-leader. Give me a chance.

When Alex reads peanut butter and jelly, I jump up. He looks at me and laughs. I knew he was joking! The class votes for eight large cheese pizzas. Alex orders a serving of anchovies on the side and offers them to anyone who dares. M.P. says she'll try one if I go first. Yuck! I follow the hairy fish with a gulp of Grape Fizzberry. To each his own! Long live democracy!

Pie in Your Eye

MAPster RULES
#1 Look for the upside.
#2 Punctuality is prime.
#3 It doesn't matter
what postion you play,
as long as you play.
#4 Complain. No gain.
#5 The best way to win over
your opponent is to put
yourself in his cleats.
#6 The greater brains,
the greater gains.